# Snow Dog, Go Dog

story by
## Deborah Heiligman

illustrated by
## Tim Bowers

SCHOLASTIC INC.

ISBN 978-0-545-68703-4

Text copyright © 2013 by Deborah Heiligman.
Illustrations copyright © 2013 by Tim Bowers. All rights reserved.
Published by Scholastic Inc., 557 Broadway, New York, NY 10012,
by arrangement with Amazon Children's Publishing. SCHOLASTIC and associated
logos are trademarks and/or registered trademarks of Scholastic Inc.

12 11 10 9 8 7 6 5 4 3 2 1          14 15 16 17 18 19/0

Printed in the U.S.A.                    40

First Scholastic printing, January 2014

The illustrations are rendered in acrylic on gessoed illustration board.
Book design by Anahid Hamparian
Editor: Margery Cuyler

For Ketzie, and for Nancy Sandberg, who found Ketzie for us

Tinka is a play dog,
a yay dog,
a loves-to-romp-all-day dog.

A fun dog,
a run dog,
a flurries-have-begun dog.

A snow dog,
a go dog,
a running-to-and-fro dog.

A where? dog,
a there! dog,

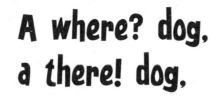

a hiding-polar-bear dog.

A hill dog,
a thrill dog,

a wibble-wobble-spill dog.

A glide dog,
a ride dog,
a body-sledding-slide dog.

Tinka is a chilly dog,
a silly dog,

a wants-to-romp-with-Millie dog.

A play dog,
a stray dog,
a wanders-far-away dog.

A chase dog,
a race dog,

a lost-in-a-strange-place dog.

Tinka is a sad dog,
a feeling-bad dog,

a wanting-what-she-had dog.

A worry dog,
a scurry dog,
a searching-in-a-hurry dog.

A joy dog!
A boy's dog!
A here's-your-favorite-toy dog!

A clomping dog,
a stomping dog,
a having-fun-and-romping dog.

Tinka is a greet dog,
a treat dog,
a being-home-is-sweet dog.

A rosy dog,
a dozy dog,
a hugged-and-fed-and-cozy dog!